Cultural Traditions in the

United Kingdom

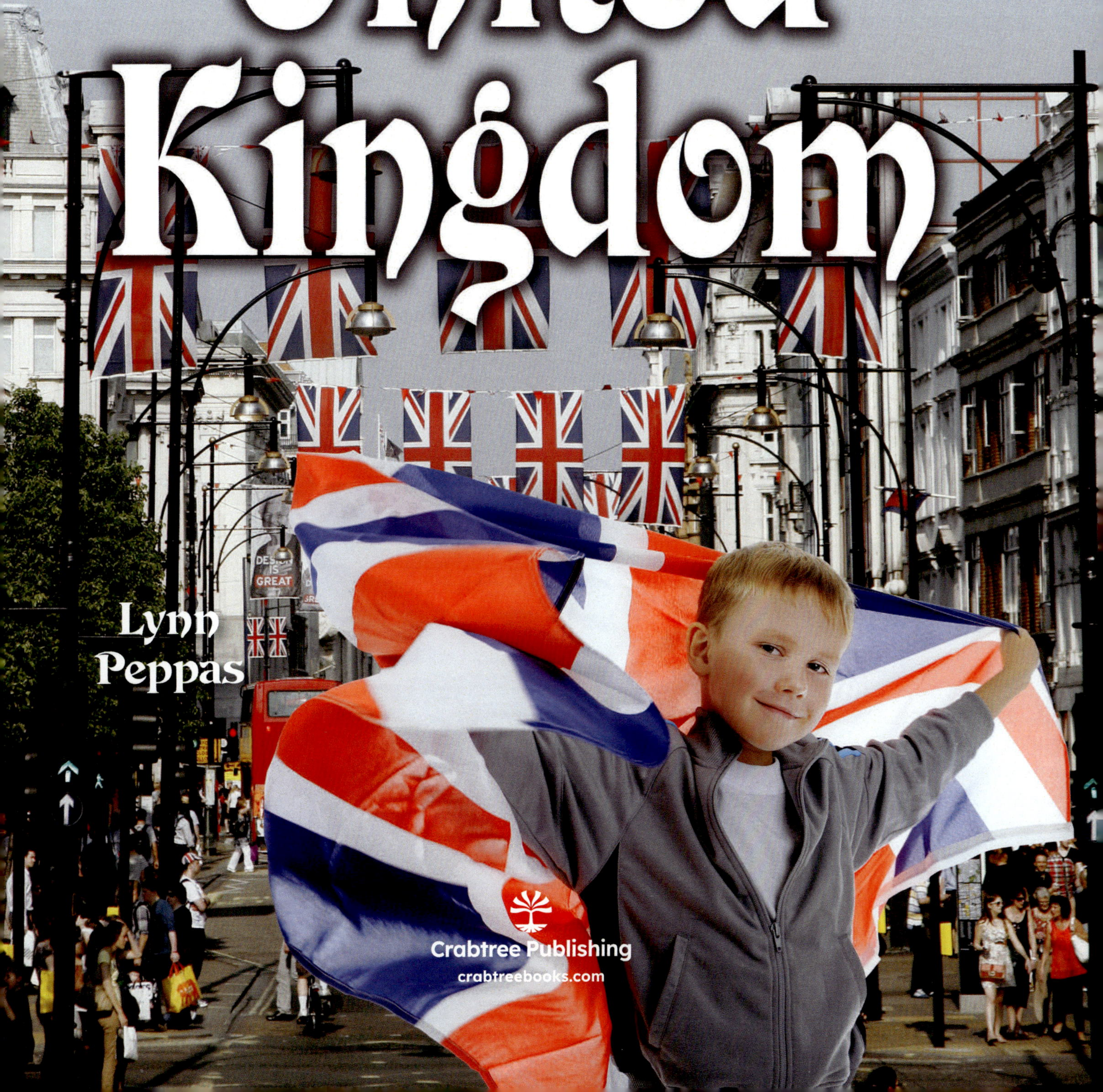

Lynn Peppas

Crabtree Publishing
crabtreebooks.com

Crabtree Publishing

crabtreebooks.com 800-387-7650

In Canada: We acknowledge the financial support of the Government of Canada through the Canada Book Fund for our publishing activities.

Author: Lynn Peppas
Publishing plan research and development: Reagan Miller
Editor: Kathy Middleton
Proofreaders: Marcia Abramson, Wendy Scavuzzo
Design: Tibor Choleva
Photo research: Melissa McClellan
Production coordinator and prepress technician: Tammy McGarr
Print coordinator: Margaret Amy Salter

Produced and Designed by BlueAppleWorks Inc.

Cover: Statue of William Shakespeare (right middle); The Big Ben, the House of Parliament and the Westminster Bridge at night, London, UK (background); Morris dancer (center); Crest Coat of Arms, UK of Great Britain & N. Ireland (bottom center); tea with scones (bottom right); Fish & Chips (bottom left); Iconic red telephone boxes in London (left middle)

Title page: Oxford Street in London

Hardcover 978-0-7787-0301-3
Paperback 978-0-7787-0313-6
Ebook (pdf) 978-1-4271-7485-7

Printed in Canada/112024/CP20241104

Library and Archives Canada Cataloguing in Publication

Peppas, Lynn, author
Cultural traditions in the United Kingdom / Lynn Peppas.

(Cultural traditions in my world)
Includes index.
Issued in print and electronic formats.
ISBN 978-0-7787-0301-3 (bound).--ISBN 978-0-7787-0313-6 (pbk.).--ISBN 978-1-4271-7485-7 (html).--ISBN 978-1-4271-7491-8 (pdf)

1. Holidays--Great Britain--Juvenile literature. 2. Great Britain--Social life and customs--Juvenile literature. I. Title. II. Series: Cultural traditions in my world

GT4843.P46 2014 j394.26941 C2014-900913-5
C2014-900914-3

Published in Canada
Crabtree Publishing
616 Welland Avenue
St. Catharines, Ontario
L2M 5V6

Published in the United States
Crabtree Publishing
347 Fifth Avenue
Suite 1402-145
New York, NY 10016

Illustrations:
Carlyn Iverson: page 26
Photographs:
Dreamstime: © Valeriy Lebedev: page 1; © Robert Wisdom: page 5; © Norman Pogson: page 13 (top, middle)
Keystone Press: PA Photos: page 7; wenn.com: page 28
Shutterstock: © Claudio Divizia: cover (middle right); © Luciano Mortula cover (background); © Maisna cover (center); © Studio DMM Photography, Designs & Art cover (bottom center); © Atiketta Sangasaeng cover (bottom right); © Shaiith cover (bottom left); © chrisdorney cover (left middle); © Bikeworldtravel: pages 1 (background), 10 (bottom), 29 (top); © Naturespixel: page 4 (top); © Stefan Ataman: page 4 (bottom); © Sean Bolt: page 6 (left); © AN NGUYEN: page 6 (right); © Atlaspix: page 8 (top); © Featureflash: pages 8 (bottom), 9; © phofotos: page 10 (top); © Stephen Finn: page 11; © photowings: page 11 (bottom); © Vaida: page 12 (left); © StockCube: page 12 (right); © Paul McKinnon: page 13 (left); © Lisa F. Young: page 14 (left); © Sandra van der Steen: page 14 (right); © Chris Green: page 16 (left); © Algol: page 16 (right); © Aduldej: page 17; © David Burrows: page 18; © Maisna: page 19 (top); © Padmayogini: page 19 (bottom); © Jiri Hera: page 20 (top); © Shaun Jeffers: page 21; © Clive Chilvers: page 23; © jan kranendonk: page 23 (bottom); © Shkvarko: page 24 (left); © Pressmaster: page 24 (right); © Becky Wass: page 25 (top); © Vietrov Dmytro: page 25 (bottom); © themorningglory: page 26 (top); © Mark Lorch: page 26 (bottom right); © Marbury: page 27 (bottom); © Lasse Kristensen: page 29 (inset); © Valentina Proskurina: page 30 (top); © Milleflore Images: page 30 (bottom); © Lesya Dolyuk: page 31 (top); © wavebreakmedia: page 31 (bottom)
SuperStock: Robert Harding Picture Library: page 22
Wikimedia Commons: Dave Farrance: page 20 (bottom); William Warby: page 27 (top); Public Domain: pages 7 (top right); 15

Library of Congress Cataloging-in-Publication Data

Peppas, Lynn.
Cultural traditions in the United Kingdom / Lynn Peppas.
pages cm -- (Cultural traditions in my world)
Includes index.
ISBN 978-0-7787-0301-3 (reinforced library binding : alk. paper) -- ISBN 978-0-7787-0313-6 (pbk. : alk. paper) -- ISBN 978-1-4271-7491-8 (electronic pdf : alk. paper) -- ISBN 978-1-4271-7485-7 (electronic html : alk. paper)
1. Holi ys--United Kingdom--Juvenile literature. 2. Festivals--United Kingdom--Juvenile literature. 3. United Kingdom--Social life and customs--Juvenile literature. I. Title.

GT4843.P46 2014
394.26941--dc23

2014005119

Contents

Welcome to the United Kingdom

The United Kingdom is made up of four different countries: England, Scotland, Wales, and Northern Ireland. The large island in the Atlantic Ocean that contains England, Scotland, and Wales is called Great Britain. Northern Ireland is the northeastern part of another large island that lies to the west of Great Britain. Each country brings its own unique language, culture, and history to the United Kingdom. Immigrants from other countries have added even more traditions to its culture.

Over 61 million people live in the United Kingdom. The British people celebrate their **culture** with holidays and festivals throughout the year. Public holidays are called bank holidays in the United Kingdom, and most people get the day off school or work. Some celebrations feature **ancient** traditions that have been followed for thousands of years. Traditions are customs that have been handed down from **ancestors**.

London is the capital city of England and the United Kingdom.

The ancestors of the English people came from groups called the Anglo-Saxons, Britons, Danes, and Normans. The Scottish and Irish people came from the Picts, Gaels, and Celts. The Welsh people came from the Celts.

Family Traditions

The early Anglo-Saxons believed family gatherings helped keep evil spirits away. Today, family celebrations are just as important to the British people as they were for their ancestors. Mothers and fathers are celebrated with their own days. Mothering Sunday is usually celebrated in March and Father's Day is in June.

Did You Know?
Birthdays for children in England often include a fortune telling cake with small objects baked inside, such as fake coins, toys, and candy. Whatever you find in your slice is what your fortune, or luck, will be. If you find a coin, for example, you will become wealthy!

Long ago carlings were served on Mothering Sunday. Carlings are peas fried in butter. Whoever ate the last pea would be the first one to marry.

Heritage often plays a large part in weddings in the United Kingdom. In Scotland, many grooms will wear a kilt, which is a kind of skirt, made from their family's tartan. A tartan is a plaid pattern designed specifically for one family. In Northern Ireland, many brides and grooms will have one hand tied to the other's with a ribbon throughout the ceremony.

In Wales, it was tradition to carve decorations onto a wooden lovespoon to give to a sweetheart.

In the 1700s, England had strict marriage laws where couples could not marry under the age of 21. Many young couples came to Gretna Green, Scotland, where the legal age to marry was 16.

The Royal Family

For over 1,000 years, **monarchs** ruled over the countries that make up the United Kingdom. Today, the monarch is still honored, but she does not **govern**, or rule, the country as kings and queens once did. Queen Elizabeth II is the current monarch. She lives at Buckingham Palace in London, England, with her family. She represents the people of the United Kingdom and takes part in traditional ceremonies.

Queen Elizabeth II and her husband, Prince Philip, make public appearances around the world. The Royal Family also works with charities to help raise money.

The wedding day of Prince William and Kate Middleton on April 29, 2011, was declared a bank holiday in the UK.

Special events in the lives of the royal family, such as weddings, births, and anniversaries, are often marked by a special holiday. In 2012, the United Kingdom celebrated Queen Elizabeth's 60th year as queen, called the Diamond Jubilee, with a four-day celebration. The Queen took part in public celebrations such as a display of boats on the Thames River, concerts, and special parties. Everyone was given the day off to hold neighborhood street parties and greet members of the royal family as they toured the United Kingdom.

Did You Know?
Many people from all over the world follow the lives of the royals such as William, Kate, and baby George.

New Year's Eve

New Year's Eve falls on December 31, the last day of the year. On New Year's Eve hundreds gather at the Thames River near the Palace of Westminster. At midnight, the palace clock tower—nicknamed Big Ben—rings in the New Year. After midnight people enjoy a colorful fireworks display to welcome the New Year!

The city of London celebrates the New Year with fireworks over the Big Ben clock tower.

New Year's Eve in Scotland is called Hogmanay. People clean their houses and pay their bills on New Year's Eve so they start the New Year fresh and **debt-free**. Scottish people take part in Hogmanay parties that last all night and well into New Year's Day. The New Year's Eve street party in Edinburgh is one of the largest New Year's celebrations in the world.

Did You Know?
First-footing is a very old tradition that's still practiced today in Scotland. A first-footer is the first person to enter a home in the New Year. A household will have good luck for the year if its first-footer brings gifts.

Hundreds of people dunk themselves in the river at the annual New Year's Day Dook in Dundee, Scotland.

Robert Burns Day

Robert Burns Day, which is also called Burns Night, is celebrated mainly in Scotland and Northern Ireland every year on or around January 25. That is the birthdate of the famous Scottish poet Robert Burns. Born in 1759 in Alloway, Scotland, Burns is known as Scotland's national poet. Scottish people celebrate their heritage on Robert Burns Day.

Scotland has many statues of Robert Burns.

These Scottish men are wearing a traditional costume called a kilt. Scottish family groups each have a unique tartan, or plaid, pattern.

Special Burns Night dinners have been held since 1802, with traditional Scottish dishes such as haggis, neeps, and tatties. Burns Night parties include readings of Robert Burns' poems and sometimes traditional Scottish dances after dinner.

Did You Know?
One of Robert Burns's most popular poems, "Auld Lang Syne," is sung by millions of people around the world on New Year's Eve!

Haggis is a dish of sheep's **organ** meats baked inside a sheep's stomach. Neeps are turnips, and tatties are mashed potatoes.

Religious Holidays and Traditions

People living in the United Kingdom come from many different cultures and practice their faith in different ways. Most people follow the **Christian** religion. The Church of England, or the Anglican Church, is the national Christian Church of England and Wales. The Presbyterian Church is the national Christian Church of Scotland. Other people in the United Kingdom observe the holidays of other religions such as **Islam** and **Judaism**.

A popular dessert to serve at Easter is simnel cake, a fruit cake made with marzipan.

The London Harness Horse Parade has been held on Easter Monday in the city of London for over 125 years.

Easter is a Christian holiday that falls in March or April each year. The Friday before Easter, called Good Friday, is a holiday for people of all faiths in the United Kingdom. Eating hot cross buns on Good Friday is an Easter tradition. Some believe it was started as a harvest tradition by the early Anglo-Saxons. They sacrificed an ox to bring a good harvest and baked a symbol of its crossed horns onto buns.

Did You Know?
It is a tradition for the king or queen to give coins called Maundy Money to citizens as an act of charity on the Thursday before Easter. This day is called Royal Maundy.

Saints' Days

Each country in the United Kingdom has its own patron saint. A patron saint is a religious figure from the past. People pray and give thanks to their patron saint and ask for future protection for their country and its people. St. George is the patron saint of England. St. David is the patron saint of Wales. Welsh people often prepare a traditional dish of beef or lamb stew called Cawl to celebrate St. David's Day on March 1.

On April 23, the English fly the flag of St. George's Cross outside homes or businesses on St. George's Day.

You do not have to be Irish to enjoy St. Patrick's Day celebrations. People from all over the world celebrate St. Patrick's Day!

St. Patrick's Day on March 17 is a public holiday in Northern Ireland. St. Patrick is one of the most well-known saints around the world. Once a slave of the Irish, he escaped but later returned to Ireland to spread Christianity. In Scotland, St. Andrew's Day is a public holiday on November 30. Celebrations often include a ceilidh, which is a gathering where couples dance in circles or in groups.

Stories about the saints

St. George slew a dragon to save a maiden.

St. Andrew's cross appeared in the sky during a battle ensuring a Scottish victory.

St. David made a hill spring up from the earth.

St. Patrick drove all the snakes out of Ireland.

May Day

May Day is an ancient holiday tradition that has been celebrated for over 1,000 years. It began as a celebration of spring when warmer weather helps crops grow. A May Day tradition in the United Kingdom that is still practiced today is Morris dancing. About eight dancers form two lines facing each other. They shake strips of cloth, bang sticks together, or ring bells as they dance. Today Morris dancing is often performed during May Day parades.

Morris dancers wear colorful, traditional costumes with ribbons hanging from them. Some wear bands of bells.

May Day festivals in the United Kingdom today still honor the very old tradition of crowning a young woman the May Queen.

Did You Know?
May Day garlands are flowers that are linked together for decoration. On May Day, many people dress up their homes, maypoles, and even themselves with garlands.

Long ago, Celtic and Anglo-Saxon people began the custom of dancing around a maypole on May Day. A maypole is a tall pole with colored ribbons attached at the top. Each dancer holds onto one of the ribbons and dances around the maypole. Today, May Day is a bank holiday in the United Kingdom and is celebrated on the first Monday in the month of May.

Spring Bank Holiday

Spring Bank Holiday may not have an exciting name, but everyone in the United Kingdom looks forward to this long weekend when the weather starts getting warmer. Although they are not observed on the same date, Spring Bank Holiday is sometimes referred to as Whit Monday after a religious celebration called Whit Monday. Christians were often **baptized** the day before Whit Monday and wore "white" clothing afterward.

In Brockworth, Gloucestershire, people compete in a downhill cheese-rolling race during the Spring Bank Holiday.

Did You Know?
In 2002 and 2012, the Spring Bank Holiday was moved to June 4 during the Queen's Golden and Diamond Jubilee celebrations. This gave the British people a four-day holiday to enjoy the Jubilees!

In 1965 the British government decided that the holiday would always fall on the last Monday in May. It is a day off work or school for most people. It gives people a long weekend to travel or enjoy activities with their families. In some places such as Endon, Staffordshire, people dress up their water wells with flowers and decorations. Young women compete to see who will be crowned the Well-Dressing Queen.

Midsummer's Day

The summer solstice is the first day of summer. If falls on June 21 and is called Midsummer's Day in England. Many believe it was an important day to early Celtic priests called Druids. Although it is not a holiday today, many people in the United Kingdom still celebrate the first day of summer with dancing at ancient sites such as Stonehenge.

Stonehenge is an ancient circle of stones in England built thousands of years ago. No one knows who built it or what it was used for.

Colorful costumes and traditional dancing are all a part of the fun at the Notting Hill Carnival.

The Summer Bank Holiday in August is the last holiday before heading back to school. Over two million people attend the Notting Hill Carnival held in London during the Summer Bank Holiday. This annual street festival celebrates the many different cultures that make up the United Kingdom. Steel drum bands and other musicians play music.

Did You Know?
Singers, actors, mimes, and other artists from all over the world perform at the Edinburgh International Festival in Scotland over the Summer Bank Holiday.

Punky Night and Halloween

Punky Night is an old tradition that began in southern parts of England such as Cornwall. Children and adults carve faces into a kind of beet called a mangel-wurzel. They place a candle inside and use it as a lantern. It is similar to the North American tradition of the jack-o'-lantern. There are "Punky" songs that people sing during the night. Punky Night is celebrated on the last Thursday in October.

Children in the United Kingdom trick-or-treat on Halloween night, the same way children from North America do!

Did You Know?
Bobbing for apples is a traditional game played at Halloween parties. Apples float in a bucket of water. Players have to grab an apple with their teeth only—no hands allowed!

Halloween is a more recent celebration in the United Kingdom. In some parts of the country children dress up in costumes and go door to door collecting treats. Halloween falls on the last day of October, the night before All Saints' Day when ghost-like spirits were believed to visit Earth. Children dress in scary costumes so the evil spirits won't recognize them. Lighting bonfires is another tradition for scaring spirits away.

Guy Fawkes Night

Guy Fawkes Night is always celebrated on November 5. It is sometimes called Bonfire Night. Guy Fawkes Night remembers an event that happened over 400 hundred years ago. Guy Fawkes took part in a plan to kill the King of England. On November 4, 1605, he filled a room underneath a government building with explosives. He planned to blow up the King and other government leaders the next day. But Fawkes was caught and the **assassination** never took place.

Guy Fawkes was captured by soldiers on the morning of November 5. He was treated cruelly in jail, then **executed** for the crime that he never got the chance to carry out.

After 1605, people wanted to show they were loyal to their King. They lit bonfires and burned straw dolls dressed as Guy Fawkes. The tradition of the bonfire continues today. People hold parties and often bake potatoes and cook other foods over the fire on Guy Fawkes Night. Fireworks displays held in large cities are a reminder of the explosives that did not kill the King that night long ago.

Today Guy Fawkes dolls are often made from paper and old clothing.

Large bonfires are lit all over the country on Guy Fawkes Night.

Remembrance Day

Remembrance Day is sometimes called Poppy Day. It used to be called **Armistice** Day, the day World War I ended. In the United Kingdom it is a day for remembering the sacrifices others made for their country during World War I and World War II. Remembrance Day is observed on November 11, the official date that World War I ended in 1918.

Queen Elizabeth and other members of the royal family lay wreaths at the Cenotaph war memorial on every Remembrance Day.

Military veterans march in Remembrance Day parades. People wear poppies on that day and the days leading up to it.

The British people first honored their soldiers by holding two minutes of silence at 11 a.m. on November 11, 1919. This tradition has been carried on each year at ceremonies that are usually held on the second Sunday in November, called Remembrance Sunday. People pin a red poppy over their heart as a symbol of their appeciation for the people who have served their country. A poppy is a red flower that grew on the battlefields in Belgium where many soldiers died in World War I.

Christmas and Boxing Day

Christmas is a religious holiday on December 25, when Christians celebrate the birth of Jesus Christ. Some people go to church services the night before Christmas, which is called Christmas Eve. On Christmas Day, families usually gather together for a large, mid-day meal. The day after Christmas is called Boxing Day in the United Kingdom. The name comes from the tradition of giving gifts in boxes to servants and poor people on December 26.

Christmas dinners often include Christmas crackers. Guests pull both ends of the paper tubes, and small presents fall out with a bang!

In the United Kingdom, Santa Claus is called Father Christmas. Many Christmas traditions came about during Queen Victoria's time. Her husband, Prince Albert, brought to England the German tradition of decorating Christmas trees. Hanging stockings and sending Christmas cards also became popular during Victoria's reign.

Did You Know?
Millions of people around the world listen each year to the Royal Christmas Message given by Queen Elizabeth on Christmas Day. The monarchs have kept this tradition since 1932.

Fruitcake and Christmas pudding are traditional desserts served in the United Kingdom.

Glossary

ancestors People in your family before you, usually further back than grandparents

ancient Related to a period long ago

assassination The killing of someone important

baptize A ceremony to officially make someone part of a Christian religion

Christian Someone who follows the teachings of Jesus Christ, whom they believe to be the Son of God

culture The beliefs, customs, and arts of a society

debt-free To not owe money to another person or an institution such as a bank

executed Put to death by the state after being found guilty of a crime

govern To make decisions about how a country is run

heritage The history, traditions, and culture of your ancestors

Islam The religion of Muslims

Judaism The religion of Jews

monarch A person who rules over a country or kingdom

organ A formation of tissues that performs a specialized task in the body such as a heart

Index